This book
belongs to

....

Puddle's Fan Pages

Here's what other children have to say about their favourite puppy and his latest adventure!

"Puddle is exactly the sort of puppy I would like to have! Reading about Puddle's adventures is the next best thing to actually being there with him."
Carmen, age 7

"The book is full of mystery and magic and I really liked the characters. I love the adventure." Hannah, age 7

"It made me excited reading the book and I wanted to read more and more!"
Megan, age 8

"Puddle found Mrs Whiskers and shared his red bow to make friends. I liked the end because Ruby's dream came true."
Lucina, age 6

"I laughed when Puddle snatched the microphone. It was so exciting when Ruby pushed the button on the space ship. I was pleased when Ruby got to meet Charisma." Isabel, age 7

"I really, really like it. It's really good because Ruby has her dream come true. My favourite bit is when Puddle gives the bow to Mrs Whiskers." Samantha, age 7

Puddle
the naughtiest puppy

Holiday Musical

Other books about
Puddle the Naughtiest Puppy:

Puddle
the naughtiest puppy

Holiday Musical

by Hayley Daze
illustrated by Ann Kronheimer
cover illustrated by Paul Hardman

A catalogue record for this book is available from the British Library

Published by Ladybird Books Ltd
A Penguin Company
Penguin Books Ltd., 80 Strand, London WC2R 0RL, UK
Penguin Books Australia Ltd., Camberwell, Victoria, Australia
Penguin Group (NZ) 67 Apollo Drive, Rosedale,
North Shore 0632, New Zealand

001 –

1 3 5 7 9 10 8 6 4 2
Series created by Working Partners Limited, London W6 0QT
Text © Working Partners Ltd MMXI
Cover illustration © Working Partners Ltd MMXI
Interior illustrations © Ladybird Books Ltd MMXI

Special thanks to Mo O'Hara

ISBN: 978-1-40930-658-0
Printed in England

Mixed Sources
Product group from well-managed
forests and other controlled sources
www.fsc.org   Cert no. SA-COC-001592
© 1996 Forest Stewardship Council

FSC

For Ava, a Puddle super-fan!

When clouds fill the sky and rain starts to fall,
Ruby and Harry are not sad at all.
They know that when puddles appear on the ground,
A magical puppy will soon be around!

Puddle's his name, and he's the one
Who can lead you to worlds of adventure and fun!
He may be quite naughty, but he's clever too,
So come follow Puddle – he's waiting for you!

A present from Puddle:

Look out for the special code at the back of the book to
get extra-special games and loads of free stuff at Puddle's
website! Come and play at www.puddlethepuppy.com

Contents

Chapter One
Red Carpet Ruby

Ruby's tin-foil tiara bounced on top of her head as she danced in front of the TV, singing along to her favourite DVD.

"Dance down the hall, you're at Hollywood High, yeah! Life is a ball here at Hollywood . . ." Ruby ran on the spot in time to the music as it built to the final note. "High!" she

yelled and leapt up into the air, her
arms stretched wide. Ruby flopped
back on to the settee in Grandad's
lounge. She stared at the girl on TV
in the sparkly cheerleader outfit. She
had dark curly hair and a little dimple
in her cheek that you could see

whenever she gave her Hollywood smile. "Isn't Charisma Carter amazing, Harry? I could watch that film a hundred times."

Ruby's cousin Harry looked up from the table. He had sticky tape in one hand and a tennis ball in the other.

"You nearly have. I think you're up to ninety-seven," he said, and pushed his glasses into place with the back of his hand.

Harry finished taping the tennis ball to the end of a cardboard tube, which came from the middle of Grandad's kitchen roll. "There, I've made you a microphone for the red carpet interview with Charisma

Carter." Harry held up his new creation.

"And I've got the red carpet," Ruby added. She rolled out a large red bath mat on the floor and stepped on to it.

"You promise that if I pretend to interview you, I can watch *Cosmic Battle Droids* next?" Harry asked.

"I promise," Ruby said. She straightened her tin-foil tiara and tied Grandad's raincoat around her shoulders like an elegant cape. "Now I'm ready to meet my fans," she said.

Harry pointed the microphone at Ruby. "So ... um ... are you excited to be making *Hollywood High Two*?" he asked.

Ruby waved to her imaginary fans. "It's a dream come true." She struck a dramatic pose like the ones she'd seen in all the glossy magazines. "You can take my picture now."

Harry picked up his mobile and used it as a camera.

Ruby could hear the rain drumming against the lounge windows, almost in time to the beat of the music coming from the TV.

Just then, the door to the garden blew open and Puddle, their magical puppy friend, rushed into the room. Puddle always arrived when it rained, and he took them on fantastic adventures. The little puppy jumped on to the pretend red carpet and shook himself dry.

"Puddle!" Ruby squealed. "We can pretend you're Mrs Whiskers."

"Is that the fluffy white cat with the silly pink tail in *Hollywood High*?" Harry asked.

Ruby nodded and scooped up Puddle. Harry held the tennis ball microphone out to the puppy. Puddle grabbed the tennis ball in his mouth, jumped down and ran straight to the garden.

"Hey, that's our microphone!"
Harry called after him. "You naughty
puppy."

"I guess it's time for another
rainy-day adventure," Ruby said, as
she took off her tiara and cape. She
giggled. "My fans will have to wait."

The cousins ran out of the door
and followed Puddle. He leapt
from puddle to puddle down the
garden path until he came to just

the right one. Ruby tugged on her plaits for luck as she, Harry and Puddle all jumped together and, with a Hollywood-sized splash, disappeared.

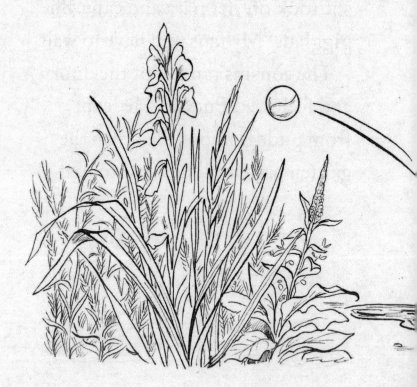

Chapter Two
Puddle to the Rescue

Ruby opened her eyes, but it was so dark she could hardly see a thing. *It can't be night-time already*, she thought. She felt around on her hands and knees, trying to work out where they were. Ruby could feel cool grass beneath her fingers. As her eyes adjusted, she saw that there were white lines painted on the grass and a goalpost sticking up in the distance.

"It looks like a playing field," Ruby said to Harry, who was crawling around next to her.

"Miaoooooooooooooooow!"

The sound startled Ruby and Harry. Puddle hunched down as if he was preparing to pounce. "Was that a cat?" Harry asked.

They heard another loud, screeching mew. Ruby thought that the cat sounded cross. If she could understand cat-speak, she was sure it would be saying, "Leave me alone!"

Ruby spotted two big boys across the field, trying to put something white into a cardboard box.

"They're kidnapping a cat," Ruby whispered.

Puddle growled quietly.

"I think technically you'd call it cat-napping," Harry said.

"Miaooooooooooooow!" the cat bellowed again. The cat swished its tail wildly from side to side.

Ruby gasped as she realized that
the cat's tail was pink. "It's Mrs
Whiskers, the Hollywood High
mascot. We have to save her!"

Harry and Ruby sprinted over
to the cat-nappers, with Puddle
right behind them. The little puppy
excitedly weaved in and out of the
boys' legs.

"Hey, what's going on?" the boy holding Mrs Whiskers yelled as he tripped over Puddle and fell backwards. Mrs Whiskers leapt on to the grass.

"Puddle to the rescue!" Ruby shouted.

"Aaaachoo!" Harry sneezed. "I'm allergic to cats," he said, snuffling.

Suddenly a booming voice called out across the field, "CUT!"

31

Bright lights lit up the playing field. Ruby rubbed her eyes. They weren't outdoors at all, but inside a huge building that had been made to look like a playing field. All around them were lights on scaffolding, men holding microphones on long poles, and big cameras on wheels.

"We're in a film studio," Harry said. "This is a film set."

"Not just any film set," Ruby added, pointing up to a banner hanging on the goalpost. "Look, Harry. It says '*Hollywood High*'!" She jumped up and down, making her plaits bounce.

"I can't believe it!" Ruby went on. "That means Charisma Carter could be here!"

Ruby was still bouncing when she felt a tap on her shoulder. She turned round to see a man in a baseball cap.

"You three ruined that shot," the man said. "Now we'll have to reshoot the whole scene." He spoke in the same kind of voice her dad had used when she'd filled up the bathtub with tadpoles.

"We're sorry," Harry said.

Then a booming voice filled the studio. Everyone stopped to listen. "Get that naughty dog and those two kids over here now!"

"Uh-oh," the man said, shaking his head. "The director wants to see you. You're in big trouble now."

Chapter Three
Catch that Puppy!

Ruby's heart pounded as she, Harry and Puddle walked across the studio to see the director. He was a large man with a beard, sitting in a canvas chair with 'Mr B' written on the back.

"Get me the writers now!" Mr B shouted into the megaphone he was holding. His voice was so loud that Puddle lay down and put his paws

over his ears. "I want to change the finale," Mr B continued. "She's out and he's in!"

"Do you mean Mrs Whiskers?"

Ruby asked. "But she didn't do anything wrong."

"That's showbiz," Mr B said and leaned back in his chair. "Your little dog has star quality. We're rewriting the finale to star your puppy. Chad!" he shouted to the assistant in the baseball cap. "Get the dog down to make-up and escort the cat off the set."

"Right away, Mr B," Chad said.

He walked over towards Puddle and held out his arms. "Here, boy!"

Puddle backed away and barked playfully. "Woof, woof!" Then he leapt right through Chad's outstretched arms and ran off.

"Puddle – come back!" Ruby called.

She, Harry and Chad followed

Puddle as he ran across the playing field and into another film set. This one looked like a school gym with basketball hoops and rows of seats.

"Hey," Ruby said as she ran,

"this is where Charisma did her big cheerleading routine in *Hollywood High*." Ruby tingled with excitement at the thought of actually meeting her idol.

They ran across the pretend basketball court and dodged past two security guards. The guards were carrying Mrs Whiskers away in her basket. Mrs Whiskers' eyes were narrowed and her pink tail swished.

Poor Mrs Whiskers, Ruby thought.

"We've nearly caught up with Puddle," Harry said. "Come on!"

Ruby, Harry and Chad chased the puppy into the next set. They ducked under a volleyball net strung across a pretend sandy beach. Ruby's plaits flew out behind her as she jumped over sandcastles. A huge photo of a golden sunset hung on the far wall.

"It's just like being on holiday,"
Ruby said.

Puddle gave a bark and bolted
around a corner, into yet another set.
Ruby, Harry and Chad hurried after
him – and skidded to a halt. They
were standing in front of a massive
silver flying saucer.

"Aliens!" Ruby shouted. Puddle
ran up the ramp into the ship.

Harry adjusted his glasses. "That's the star cruiser from the film *Cosmic Battle Droids Five*."

"It certainly is," Chad said, panting. "Now, let's get on board and catch that puppy."

They hurried up the ramp. Inside, Puddle was standing on a narrow bridge over a glowing green pool that reflected the silver walls of the spaceship. At the front of the flying

saucer was a gleaming control panel
and seats for the crew. Ruby walked
over and stared at all the flashing
lights and red buttons. She was dying
to push one, just to see what it did.

Harry pointed to the green pool.
"That's the ship's energy core," he

said. "I've seen the film fourteen times."

Puddle sat down in the centre of the bridge.

"We need to get him down from there," Chad said. He started to cross the bridge towards Puddle as Harry crept up the other side.

Ruby was reading the labels by the buttons on the control panel. "'Air lock', 'Laser rays'," she read out loud. "Oh, this red button says 'Energy core'. I wonder what it does." She pushed it.

All the lights on the control panel started to flash. The bridge Puddle, Harry and Chad were standing on

tilted down, making them lurch
towards the green pool.

Ruby's eyes opened wide. "Oh no!"
she said, realizing that she shouldn't
have pushed the red button.

"Whoa!" Harry yelled. He and
Chad slid off the bridge, splashing
Ruby with green goo.

"Ruff, ruff!" Puddle barked, his
paws skittering as he tried to stay

upright.

"Puddle, I'll save you!" Ruby shouted as the little puppy toppled over the side. She lunged forward and caught him in her outstretched arms. "Got you!" she said, cuddling Puddle close. But her feet were slipping and sliding. She was heading straight for the glowing green pool!

Chapter Four
Sequins and Soap Bubbles

With a gloopy, slurping noise, Ruby and Puddle sank for a second into the green slime and then bobbed up and poked their heads above the surface. Ruby wiped her eyes and spotted Harry and Chad, who now looked like green aliens.

Harry touched the tip of his tongue to the jiggling goo. "It's jelly," he said.

Ruby licked her lips. "Mmmm," she said. "Lime flavour, my favourite."

Puddle wriggled out of Ruby's arms and paddled around the pool, barking happily.

Chad was fishing around for his baseball cap. "I had no idea Puddle was such a great stunt dog. All that running and leaping through the film sets – wow!"

"Do you still want Puddle to be in the film?" Ruby asked, crossing her sticky, jelly-coated fingers.

"Of course," Chad said, putting his squelchy cap back on. "But I know that, as his trainers, you want to keep a close eye on him."

"Trainers?" Harry asked.

Ruby elbowed Harry.

"You could be in the big finale with Puddle," Chad said.

Harry scratched his sticky head.

He didn't look sure about Chad's suggestion. Ruby gave him one of her 'please, please, with marshmallows and sprinkles on top' kind of looks.

Harry sighed. "Okay."

"Yaaaay!" Ruby shouted.

"Woof, woof!" Puddle barked, as if he was pleased too. He licked a big drip of lime jelly from Ruby's chin.

Chad grinned. "Let's go and
get cleaned up – and get you your
Hollywood High costumes!"

They all climbed out of the jelly
and dripped and blobbed their way
to the make-up trailer, leaving gooey
green footprints as they went. Inside

the trailer was a long dressing table
with a row of mirrors above it, which
were surrounded by bright lights.
On the table were boxes of wigs and
make-up, and leaning against the
opposite wall was a rack of costumes.
Ruby and Harry splashed in the sink
until they were clean.

Chad rummaged through the costumes and pulled out a sparkly cheerleader outfit for Ruby and a rainbow-coloured basketball uniform for Harry. Ruby ran her fingers over the sequinned fabric. She couldn't believe she was going to be wearing it in a real Hollywood film.

"Aaachooo!" Harry sneezed. "I think Mrs Whiskers must be in this trailer somewhere," he said, blowing his nose.

"Mrs Whiskers isn't on the set any more," Chad said. "Remember, we saw her being carried away. It must be something else that's making you sneeze."

Puddle wagged his tail and a blob of green jelly flew off the end.

"Let's get you cleaned up too," Ruby said to Puddle. She scooped him up from the dressing table, but before she could gently place him in the tub, the little puppy leapt from her arms and dived right in – just as if he was diving into one of his magical puddles. *Splash!* The soapy water and suds flew everywhere.

"Puddle, you naughty puppy," Ruby said, between giggles. "Oh well, at least Harry and I will be really clean now."

Bang, bang, bang!

Someone was knocking on the door, so forcefully that it made the trailer shake. Ruby opened it to reveal Mr B standing outside with a bundle of paper.

"This is the script for the new finale of the movie," Mr B said, handing Ruby the freshly printed pages.

"It's the only copy," he shouted as he hurried away. "Learn your parts fast. We're filming the finale today."

Ruby stared at the stack of pages. There were cues for Puddle to bark and dance moves for her and Harry. There was so much to remember!

"See you on set," Chad said with a smile as he followed Mr B back towards the film set. As Ruby waved goodbye she saw the door of the trailer next to theirs open. Out stepped a girl dressed in a cheerleader outfit.

"It's her!" Ruby squealed. "It's Charisma Carter!" Ruby was fizzing with excitement as she leapt down from the trailer and ran up behind the girl. Ruby tapped her on the shoulder, and in a quivery voice said, "Charisma?"

Chapter Five
Pampered Puddle

Ruby was going to meet her all-time
favourite film star. She smoothed
her plaits. The girl tossed her long
hair over one shoulder as she turned
slowly to face Ruby. Ruby's tummy
turned somersaults. The girl smiled,
and Ruby saw that she didn't have the
little dimple in her cheek.

"Wait, you're not Charisma

Carter," Ruby said, puzzled.

The girl shook her head. "I'm Charisma's stand-in."

Ruby put her hands on her hips. "What do you mean? Charisma can stand. I've seen her do it a hundred times."

"No, I mean I'm Charisma's lookalike, her double," the girl said. "I stand in for her in certain shots so she doesn't have to be on set the whole time."

"I would love to be Charisma's stand-in," Ruby said. "It must be so much fun."

"It is," the girl agreed. "I've finished my scenes now. So I'm going home. Charisma will be in the finale."

The girl waved goodbye, and Ruby cartwheeled all the way back to the make-up trailer. So she would get to meet Charisma today, after all!

When Ruby entered the trailer, Puddle was happily being fussed

over by the make-up lady. She had
brushed Puddle's fur so that it was
really fluffy and had even added extra
spots to his coat with make-up. She
had given the little puppy a bone to
chew on while she tied a big red bow
around his neck.

Harry had on his basketball
costume and was trying to get Puddle
to learn his part in the finale. He read

out Puddle's cues again and again,
but Puddle was too busy chewing his
bone to pay attention.

Suddenly an announcement came
over the loudspeaker. "Puddle, Ruby
and Harry, make your way to the gym
set, please!"

"Aaachoo!" Harry sneezed,
dropping the script on to the dressing
table while he blew his nose.

This is it! Ruby thought as she
slipped into the bathroom and
changed into her cheerleader outfit.

Ruby, Harry and Puddle hurried
out of the trailer, then Ruby suddenly
remembered the script Mr B had
given them. She bounded back up

the steps and looked on the dressing table where she had seen Harry drop it. But the script wasn't there.

Harry must already have it, she thought, and hurried to the gym set. The set was crowded with boys and girls, all wearing basketball and cheerleader outfits just like Ruby's

and Harry's. Ruby scanned the set for Charisma Carter, but she couldn't see her anywhere.

"Harry," Ruby said, "have you got the script? I want to practise with Puddle."

"No. I thought you had it," Harry said with a frown.

71

Chad strode up to the cousins. "You certainly look the part now," he said, smiling as he admired their costumes. Puddle barked. "You too, Puddle," he added, bending down to pat Puddle's head.

Chad ushered Ruby and Puddle to the chorus line of cheerleaders and led Harry to the basketball hoops.

The cheerleaders were practising their dance routine, kicking their legs high and waving fluffy pompoms. Ruby copied their moves.

"Yip! Yip! Yip!" Puddle yapped. He skittered in and out of the cheerleaders' legs.

"Puddle, don't be so naughty," Ruby said, but she couldn't help giggling as she scolded him.

"You have no idea how naughty that puppy really is!" a voice boomed across the set.

It was Mr B. Everyone fell silent as

he stormed over to Ruby and Puddle. He was waving a mess of torn papers in his hand. "Look what he's done!" he fumed. "Your dog has shredded the only copy of the new script – now we won't be able to shoot the finale. *Hollywood High Two* has been ruined by your naughty puppy!"

Chapter Six
Paw Print Puzzle

The actors and film crew all turned
to look at Puddle. They tutted
and shook their heads. Puddle
whimpered and pawed at Ruby's
ankle socks. Harry ran over to stand
beside them.

"I know it wasn't you, boy," Ruby
said. She turned to Mr B. "Puddle
just wouldn't do that."

"Then how do you explain his paw prints on the shredded pages?" Mr B asked. He handed the ruined script to the cousins.

An announcement blared out from the loudspeaker. "Miss Charisma Carter is on her way to the set!"

Mr B bellowed into his megaphone, "Not now! Thanks to these three, Miss Carter will have to wait." He turned to Harry, Ruby and Puddle. "I want all of you off my set!"

Ruby blinked back a tear. She had been so excited about meeting her favourite actress, and now they were being kicked off the set.

"Wait, Mr B," Harry shouted.

"Look at this." He pointed to the green gooey tracks that Puddle had left on the floor after falling into the slime in the spaceship.

"Your naughty puppy has ruined the floor too," Mr B said.

Harry knelt down next to the sticky prints. "Look. These are Puddle's paw prints on the gym floor. They're not the same as the paw prints on the shredded script."

Ruby looked closely at the gooey green prints. "You're right, Harry. The ones on the page are smaller, so they can't be Puddle's. They must belong to . . ."

"Mrs Whiskers!" Ruby, Harry and Chad all said together.

Puddle barked and rubbed up against Harry's leg.

"Mrs Whiskers must be upset at being left out of the final scene," Ruby said. "Mr B, if we can find Mrs Whiskers, will you let her and Puddle both be in the finale?"

Mr B rubbed his beard. "If it helps to get this film finished, then yes. But if you don't find her quickly, we

won't have time to shoot the final
scene." He leaned down and tickled
Puddle's ears. "I'm sorry I blamed
you, Puddle."

Harry tapped Mr B on the
shoulder. "I think I can remember
a lot of the final scene," he said.
"I practised it over and over with
Puddle."

Mr B slapped Harry on the back.
"Harry and I will rewrite the script,

while Ruby and Puddle get that cat!"

Puddle gave the script a sniff, then raced across the set.

"He's following Mrs Whiskers' scent," Ruby shouted as she ran after him.

The cheerleaders and basketball players clapped and cheered. "Go Ruby!" they chanted. "Go Puddle!"

Puddle raced through the different film sets, snuffling the air as he went.

Ruby followed him as he climbed up
an Egyptian pyramid, jumped on to
a circus's big top, and ran through an
ice cream parlour – only stopping for
one lick of ice cream. They followed
Mrs Whiskers' scent all the way to

one of the trailers.

Puddle pawed at the door and barked. Ruby read the swirly letters painted on it: CHARISMA CARTER.

Ruby tugged on her plaits for luck as she knocked on the door. This was the moment she had been waiting for. She was finally going to meet Charisma Carter!

Chapter Seven
Lights, Camera, Action!

Ruby heard a crash from inside the
trailer. She flung open the door
and rushed in. A costume rack had
toppled over. Ruby knelt down and
searched through the tangled pile of
sequinned skirts, colourful T-shirts
and frilly scarves. Puddle pushed
his nose among them and dug with
his paws.

"Charisma?" Ruby asked. "Is that you?"

"Miaoooow!" The sound came from where Puddle was digging.

Ruby spotted a twitching pink tail. She lifted a purple dress to find a white cat crouching beneath it, bits of shredded paper sticking out of her mouth.

"Mrs Whiskers," Ruby said with a sigh. She gently pulled the bits of paper away.

Ruby looked around the empty trailer. "Charisma must already be on her way to the set. Come on, Mrs Whiskers – we have to get there for the finale."

But the cat turned away from her and curled up into a ball.

"I'm sorry that you got left out of
the film because of us," Ruby said,
stroking the fluffy white cat.

Puddle nuzzled up against Mrs
Whiskers. He wriggled out of his red
bow and pushed it towards her. Mrs
Whiskers started to purr.

 Ruby clapped
her hands in
delight. "You two
are going to look
great together in
the final scene," she said, as she tied
the bow around Mrs Whiskers' neck.

Ruby ran back to the set with Mrs
Whiskers and Puddle trotting right
behind. Mr B beamed when he saw

them. Chad took Puddle and Mrs
Whiskers to their positions on set.

Ruby looked around for Charisma.
There she was, right at the front!
Ruby's heart started thumping so
loudly she thought it would drown
out the music. *It's her! It's really her!*
she thought.

Ruby weaved her way among the
cast and crew towards Charisma.

With every step, Ruby got more nervous. She felt as if she was a firework ready to explode.

"Everyone take your places for the finale," Mr B's voice boomed over his megaphone. Ruby was so close to meeting Charisma, but she was swept away by everyone rushing to their places for the final scene.

Ruby found her place in the chorus line, right at the back. She stood on her tiptoes so she could keep Charisma in sight.

Chad stood in front of the camera with a black-and-white clapperboard and read it aloud: "*Hollywood High Two*, the finale, take one." Chad slapped the clapperboard shut.

Mr B lifted his megaphone and called, "Lights, camera, action!"

The music started and the whole place came alive. As Ruby jumped and twirled, she felt like a real Hollywood star.

Then it was Puddle and Mrs Whiskers' big moment. They dashed to the microphones that had been set at the perfect height for a puppy and a cat. As Charisma started to sing, they mewed and barked along, even wagging their tails to the beat. The music swelled to the final notes as

everyone sang together: "Life is a ball here at Hollywood ..." – Charisma jumped into her mid-air split and landed right between Puddle and Mrs Whiskers – "... High!"

Charisma patted Puddle and Mrs Whiskers and then said her final line: "Now, that's what I call a Hollywood ending!" She flashed a dazzling Charisma Carter smile right to the camera.

"Cut! That's a wrap!" Mr B yelled into his megaphone.

Chapter Eight
A Dream Come True

Everyone cheered. Ruby tried to squeeze past Mr B and the others so she could see Charisma. But Ruby was shorter than most of the people there, and she couldn't see Charisma anywhere.

"Great work, Mrs Whiskers!" Mr B said. "I've always said this cat had star quality, haven't I, Chad? Hey,

we could do another film together –
Hollywood Kitty. What do you think?"

"Woof, woof!" Ruby heard. She
turned around and Puddle jumped
into her arms.

"Oh, Puddle, you were terrific!"
Ruby said, ruffling the puppy's fur.

Puddle jumped down and started
to run around Ruby's legs.

"Puddle, do we have to go now? I'll
never get to meet Charisma." Ruby
sighed.

Just then, the crowd parted and
Harry and Charisma strode over to
Ruby and Puddle. Puddle skidded to
a halt, bumping into Charisma's leg.

"Hello, Puddle," Charisma said

with her Hollywood smile. "And hello, Ruby! Harry filled me in on everything you've done today."

Ruby had imagined what she might say at this moment: *Hi, Charisma. I'm Ruby, your number one fan.* But all that came out was, "Hhhhh..." Ruby stood there with her mouth open, staring at Charisma.

"I've never seen Ruby at a loss for

words," Harry said with a smile.

Charisma gave Ruby a big hug. "That's for saving our movie," she said. "We couldn't have finished it without you." She turned to Harry and Puddle. "And of course you too, Harry, and Puddle."

Puddle rolled over and let Charisma rub his tummy.

Ruby pinched herself to make sure

this was really happening. "Ouch!" she said, louder than she'd meant to. "I mean, wow! Thanks."

Charisma gave them her dimpled smile. "It was really great to meet you." As she walked away, she called back over her shoulder. "Ruby, I love your hair. I think I'll have plaits like that for my next movie."

"Wow!" was all that Ruby could say.

Puddle ran around Harry and Ruby's legs, faster and faster until the set started to go blurry. Mr B, Chad and the cast and crew waved goodbye and cheered as Ruby felt that familiar fizzy feeling in her tummy that meant they were on their way home. The world spun in circles until at last they were back in Grandad's garden. Ruby and Harry looked around for Puddle.

"Where has that naughty puppy disappeared to now?" Ruby smiled.

"Woof, woof!" Puddle barked as he bounded towards the cousins, holding something in his mouth. He dropped a clapperboard in front of Ruby and wagged his tail.

"It's just like being on a film set," Ruby said as she ruffled Puddle's ears.

Puddle barked again and ran off, disappearing behind Grandad's shed.

"Well, not quite the same," Harry

said as he read what was written
on the clapperboard. "Puddle the
Naughtiest Puppy."

Ruby slapped the clapperboard
shut, just as she had seen Chad do.

"That's a wrap!" Harry shouted, his
hands cupped around his mouth like
a director's megaphone.

"At least until the next rainy day,"
Ruby said, and smiled her biggest
film-star smile.

Did you enjoy Puddle's adventure?
If so, you might enjoy reading
about a little kitten called Cuddle!
Read on for the first chapter of
Cuddle's first adventure,
Magical Friends . . .

Cuddle the cutest kitten

Magical Friends

As if by magic, a grinning face framed by springy brown curls popped above Grace's garden fence. Then, in a flash, it was gone. Grace rubbed her eyes. Maybe she was so lonely she was making up imaginary friends.

The curly head appeared again, bobbing along the fence. Two hands gripped the top of the wooden slats and then the smiling face looked over.

"I'm Olivia," the curly-haired girl said.

"My mum says you're our new neighbour."

"Hi," Grace replied. "I'm Grace." Her smile was as bright as her yellow hair.

Olivia stood on tiptoes and peered further over the fence. Grace's garden had a sandpit, a bench, and a vegetable patch filled with juicy tomatoes and stringy beans. But Olivia was staring at a triangular pile of boxes in the middle of the lawn.

"Nice pyramid," she said.

"Oh – thanks," Grace replied. "These are the removal boxes Mum and Dad have unpacked."

She grabbed a box and placed it on the top of the pyramid. "I used to live on a farm. It's funny seeing so many tall buildings around here, so I thought I'd make one myself!"

The sky above them darkened as grey clouds glided across the sun.

"Is it always cloudy in Catterton?" Grace asked.

Olivia nodded. "Pretty much. But don't worry, it doesn't mean we can't have fun. We can play dressing-up indoors or chase rainbows in the garden. The best thing about living here is that there's always someone to play with." She smiled. "You just have to know where to look."

Olivia dropped down behind the fence, out of sight. Grace jumped as high as her trainers would take her, but it looked like Olivia's back garden was empty. She had vanished.

"Close your eyes," Olivia called.

Grace squeezed her eyes shut.

"Ta-dah!" Olivia said. Grace's eyes
snapped open. Olivia was standing right
in front of her.

"How did you do that?" Grace asked.
"It's like magic!"

Olivia's curls bounced as she shook her
head. "It's not magic," she said, taking
Grace's hand. "But it can be our secret!"

Olivia showed her a section of the fence
that was partly hidden by a rose bush. One
of the panels of wood was hanging loose
at the bottom. Olivia pulled it so it swung
upwards, making a gap just big enough
to squeeze through. "It's like a giant cat

flap," Grace said as she peeked into Olivia's garden.

Olivia laughed. "You're right! Miss Nancy, the old lady who used to live in your house, had seven cats. We made the flap in the fence so I could come and play with them."

Grace's mouth fell open.

"Seven cats?"

"I wish I could have just one cat," Olivia sighed. "But my dad's allergic to them. He used to start sneezing if he even looked at one of Miss Nancy's cats."

"I can't have one either," Grace said. "I've got a new baby brother. Mum says I have to wait until he's older."

Olivia sat down on the bench, her

shoulders slumped. The garden felt empty without Miss Nancy's cats. "What should we do now?" she asked her new friend.

"I know! Let's see how far we can climb up that tree." Grace pointed to the apple tree at the foot of the garden.

Olivia straightened her spotless denim skirt. "I'm not really dressed for climbing. But we could play movie-star makeover. I'm going to be an actress one day, so I've got everything we need."

She opened the sequinned bag that was always slung across her shoulder and took out a hairbrush and some sparkly hairgrips.

A sudden burst of brightness made

both girls shield their eyes. The grey clouds drifted apart and a sunbeam shone down on to Grace's garden. It showered the cardboard pyramid with sparkling golden light.

Jingle jangle jingle.

"Did you hear that?" Grace asked. "It sounded like a bell."

"Look!" Olivia shouted and pointed to Grace's cardboard tower. Sitting at the top of the pyramid, her eyes narrowed in the sunlight, was the cutest kitten either of the girls had ever seen.

***

To find out what happens next, get your copy of MAGICAL FRIENDS! Coming soon.

Magic Mayhem

Ruby and Harry are amazed to find themselves in a medieval castle...

...when Puddle takes them on their latest adventure! They meet a magician's apprentice who is in deep trouble. He's lost his spell book. Can Puddle save the day?

Find out in MAGIC MAYHEM...

Pirate Surprise

Can you imagine what it's like to sail on a pirate ship?

Ruby and Harry find out – when Puddle takes them on an amazing adventure on the high seas! Captain Redbeard has a bad case of the hiccups! Will Puddle be able to cure him?

Find out in PIRATE SURPRISE ...

Animal Antics

Join Puddle, Ruby and Harry
at the Safari Rescue Park!

All the animals
have problems they
need to overcome
before they can be
released into the
wild. Will Puddle
be able to help the
monkey who is
afraid of heights?

Find out in ANIMAL ANTICS…

Puddle
the naughtiest puppy

Christmas
Snow Puppy

Go on a festive adventure with
Ruby, Harry and Puddle!

The children find
themselves in a
beautiful winter
wonderland. Can
they get through
the snow to the
big winter festival
on time?

Find out in CHRISTMAS SNOW PUPPY ...

Star of the School

Join Puddle, Ruby and Harry
for a trip to the Wild West!

Lil the littlest
cowgirl is told she
is too small to join
the cowboy school.
But with Puddle's
help, can she prove
herself by catching
Outlaw Pete?

Find out in STAR OF THE SCHOOL...

Staying Safe Around Dogs

Hi! It's Ruby and Harry again with Puddle the puppy! Wow, haven't all our adventures just been fantastic fun?

We have also learnt so much about dogs with our friends at **Dogs Trust** – can you remember these important points about what is involved in owning a real dog?

6 Top Tips to Stay Safe:
- I ask the owner if I can stroke their dog
- I hold out my hand and let the dog sniff me
- I speak softly to the dog
- I pat the dog gently
- I play nicely
- I should sometimes leave dogs alone

Always remember, Puddle is a magical dog, while real dogs and puppies are living animals who need a lot of care, love and attention.

What Owning a Dog Involves

- **Walking** – dogs need walks to keep them nice and healthy and to stop them getting bored!
- **A dog's needs** – food, drink, lots of love and what else? Can you remember?
- **Training** – a school for dogs where they learn how to behave well is so important. It's just like you going to school!
- **A place to rest** – dogs need somewhere safe and warm to sleep and relax.
- **Playtime** – dogs love playing just as much as we do, especially with special doggy toys!
- **Regular check-ups** – at the vet, to make sure they are strong and healthy.

The most important thing to remember is that a dog has needs just like you and me and can be a truly loving and fun member of any family!

Remember, "A dog is for life, not just for Christmas®" Dogs Trust has 18 Rehoming Centres around the UK and Ireland. To find out more please go to:
www.dogstrust.org.uk
For more fun and games please go to:
www.learnwithdogs.co.uk

DogsTrust

Movie Mix-up!

Look at the strange words below.
Can you unscramble each one to make
the name of a character from the story?
Then match each word to a picture.

1. Dach
2. Harismac
3. Msr Weshkirs
4. Rm B
5. Bury

Spot the Difference!

Study the picture of Ruby and Harry below and then look at the one on the opposite page. Can you spot six tricky differences?

Answers on the next page

Answers to Puddle Puzzles:
Movie Mix-up: 1. D, Chad; 2. A, Charisma; 3. B, Mrs Whiskers;
4. E, Mr B; 5. C, Ruby
Spot the Difference: Harry's sock is black, the chair has gone,
Ruby's socks are longer, Ruby's pocket is black, the picture frame
has gone, the tennis ball is black.

For more magical adventures, come and play with Puddle at

www.puddlethepuppy.com

Use this special code to get extra special games and free stuff at puddlethepuppy.com

CLAPPERBOARD